For m,
Claire and Mere...
-KDC

Pat the Bat

Early Reader Series
Book 1

MacLaren-Cochrane Publishing, Inc.

Text © 2016 Kent Chapman
Cover and Interior Art © 2016 Kelly Stribling Sutherland

Pat the Bat Dyslexic Edition

MCPinfo@maclaren-cochranepublishing.com

Library of Congress Control Number TX 8-341-131

2nd Edition
ISBN
Hardcover: 978-1-64372-058-6
Softcover: 978-1-64372-059-3

For orders, visit
www.maclaren-cochranepublishing.com
www.facebook.com/maclaren cochrane
www.mcp-store.com

For my parents who
encouraged me in art.
-KSS

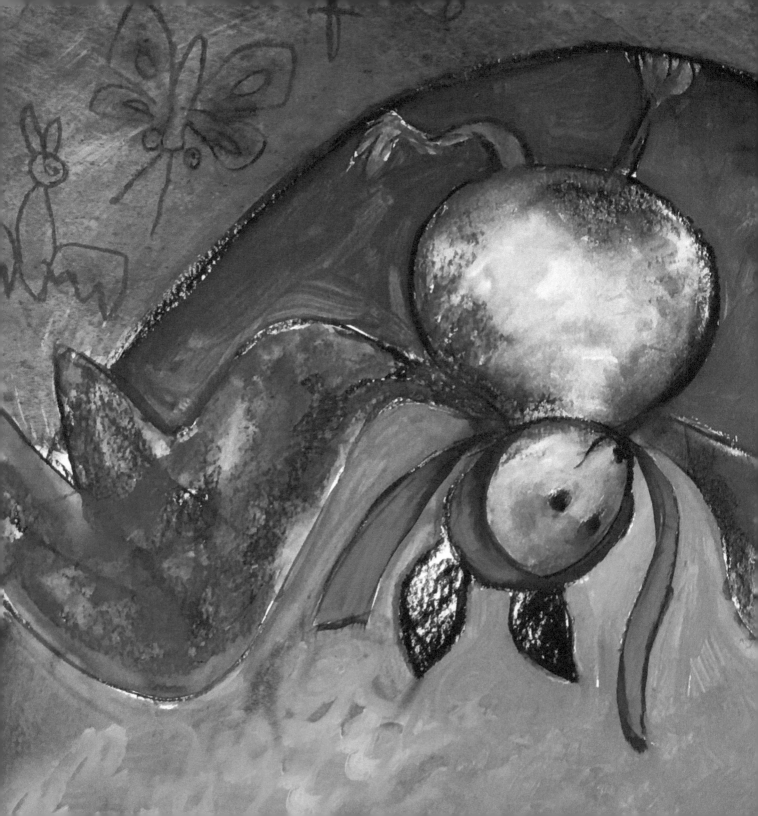

This is Pat.
Pat is a bat.

Pat is fat.
He is a fat bat.

Pat has a hat.
The hat is tall.

Pat has a cat.
The cat is small.

The cat runs
after the rat.

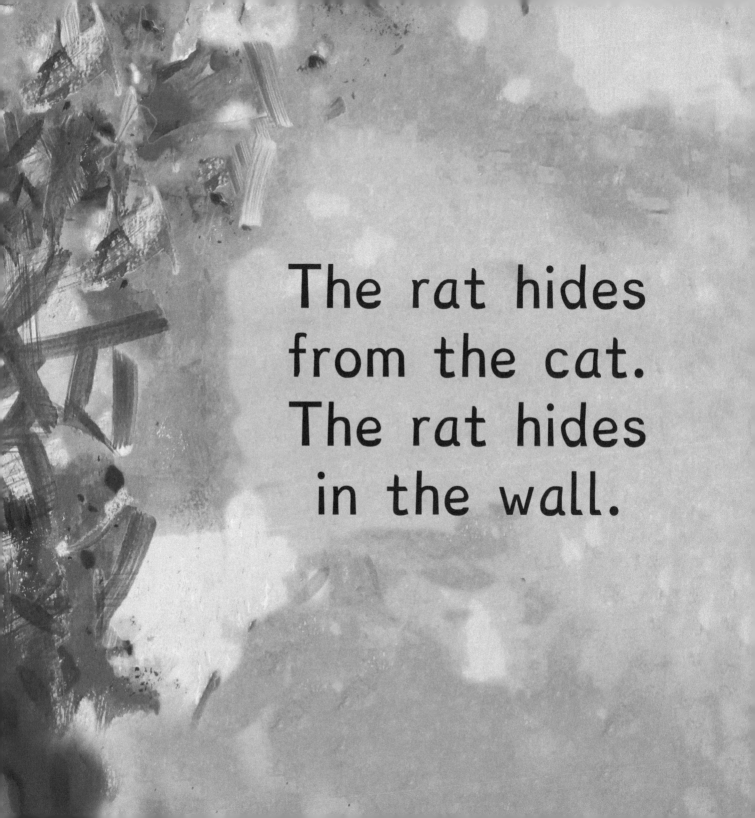

The rat hides
from the cat.
The rat hides
in the wall.

Pat flies
after
his cat.

Pat and his cat
walk home

Pat takes
a nap.

His cat takes
a nap.

Pat and his cat
dream about
the rat.

The rat takes a nap.
The rat dreams about
Pat and his cat.

The rat hopes Pat and his cat will be his new friends.

Look for

"Nat the Rat"

CPSIA information can be obtained
at www.ICGtesting.com
Printed in the USA
BVHW051550211221
624588BV00002B/166

* 9 7 8 1 6 4 3 7 2 0 5 9 3 *